Meet Ella

For Sophia – RM

For Jo, Jason, Cameron and Deborah – DM

Scholastic Australia
An imprint of Scholastic Australia Pty Limited (ABN 11 000 614 577)
PO Box 579 Gosford NSW 2250
www.scholastic.com.au

Part of the Scholastic Group
Sydney · Auckland · New York · Toronto · London · Mexico City
· New Delhi · Hong Kong · Buenos Aires · Puerto Rico

Published by Scholastic Australia in 2022.

NATIONAL LIBRARY OF AUSTRALIA
A catalogue record for this book is available from the National Library of Australia

ISBN: 978-1-76120-428-9

The illustrations in this book were created digitally.
Typeset in KG Neatly Printed and Delius.
Design by Sofya Karmazina.

Printed in China by Hang Tai Printing Company Limited.

MIX Paper FSC FSC® C023121
This product is made of material from well-managed FSC®-certified forests, recycled materials, and other controlled sources.

26 27 28 29 30 / 2

Meet Ella

Ballet Class

Rebecca McRitchie · Danielle McDonald

A Scholastic Australia Book

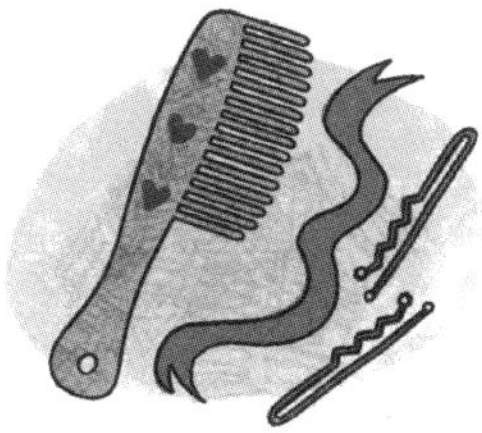

CHAPTER ONE

Meet Ella. She is six years old. Ella likes **pink shoes** and **brushing** her hair. Ella doesn't like falling over or being late.

Today is Ella's first ballet class.

Ella puts on her special ballet clothes. She wears

a stretchy, pink **leotard** and a floaty skirt that is good for **twirling**.

She has a new pair
of ballet shoes.
They are pink
and **sparkly**.

Mum brushes Ella's hair
into a bun. It matches Ella's
photo of Nana Kate.

Ella wants to be a ballerina
just like Nana Kate was.

'Ready for class, Ella?' Mum asks.

'Yes,' Ella says. But Ella is **nervous**.

Ella has never done ballet before. And Ella doesn't know anybody in her ballet class.

Her best friend, Zoe, doesn't do ballet. She plays **soccer**.

Mum drives Ella to Mrs Fry's School of Ballet.

Ella is **quiet** on the car ride.

'Ballet will be lots of fun,' Mum says. 'You'll see!'

'I wish Zoe was doing it with me,' Ella says.

Ella's tummy **flips** and **flops**.

CHAPTER TWO

Inside, there are **ballerinas** everywhere. Some ballerinas are Ella's age. Some ballerinas are older. Ella takes a deep breath.

There is a room with a big mirror on the wall. In the room, three older girls are dancing on their tippytoes! A boy ballerina **jumps** high in the air.

Wow, Ella thinks as she watches them. *Maybe one day that will be me?*

A lady wearing a black **tutu** walks over. She has her hair in a bun just like Ella.

'Hello, I am Mrs Fry,' the lady says. 'Are you a new ballerina?'

Ella nods.

'Six-year-old ballerinas,' says Mrs Fry, 'come this way, please.'

'That's you, Ella. Have fun,' Mum says. She squeezes Ella's hand.

Ella follows Mrs Fry into the room with the big mirror.

There are six ballerinas
in her class. Ella **smiles** at
them. They don't smile back.

Mrs Fry stands at the front of the room. 'Welcome to ballet,' Mrs Fry says. 'Before we dance, we must stretch.'

Mrs Fry puts her long legs out and **bends**.

Ella copies Mrs Fry. She tries not to look at herself in the big mirror.

Next, Mrs Fry **stretches** her arms behind her back. Ella does the same.

For every stretch, Ella copies Mrs Fry carefully.

'That was our **warm up**,' says Mrs Fry. 'Now the fun begins!'

CHAPTER THREE

'Now we are going to practise our ***plies***,' Mrs Fry says.

Ella doesn't know what a *plie* is.

Mrs Fry **bends** her legs very slowly.

The other ballerinas bend their legs slowly too.

'Try this,' Mrs Fry says.

Then Mrs Fry **twirls** in front of them. One twirl, two twirls, three twirls.

'Now, your turn,' Mrs Fry says.

Everybody twirls. Ella does too. But she twirls too fast. She **wibbles** and **wobbles** and then—

'Ah!' Ella cries as she falls over.

Everyone looks at Ella. Ella feels her cheeks go red. She quickly stands up.

'Like this, Ella,' Mrs Fry says. She twirls. One twirl, two twirls, three twirls.

It looks **easy** when Mrs Fry does it.

Ella tries again. She **twirls**.
One twirl, two twirls—

'Oof!' Ella **falls over** again.

'Keep practising, Ella,'
Mrs Fry says.

Ella watches
everyone else
in the class twirl.
Nobody falls over.

Ballet isn't as fun as Ella thought it was going to be. *Maybe I'm not meant to be a ballerina*, Ella thinks.

CHAPTER FOUR

At home, Ella is **upset**.

She throws down her ballet bag and **stomps** over to the couch.

'I'm not very good at ballet,' Ella says.

'You've only had one class,' Mum says.

'I couldn't **twirl** like everybody else,' Ella says. 'And I fell over. Twice.'

Ella feels **tears** in her eyes.

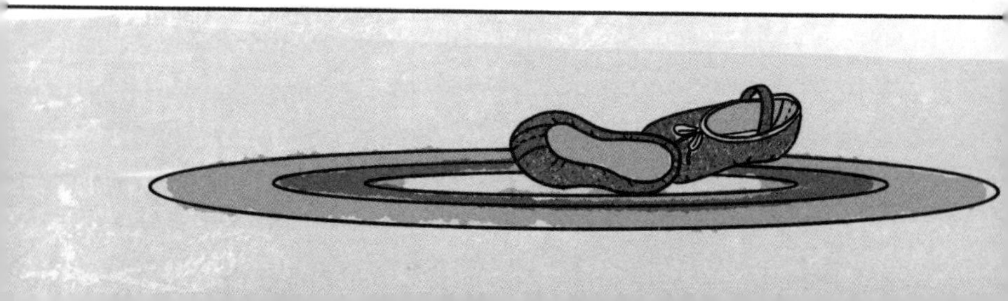

'I'll never be a ballerina like Nana Kate,' Ella says. She takes off her ballet shoes and tosses them onto the floor.

‘Nana Kate practised her ballet **every day**,’ says Mum.

'Every day?' Ella says. 'That's . . . all the days!'

'It's **hard work**,' Mum says. 'Zoe practises soccer, doesn't she?'

Ella nods. Ella really wants to be good at ballet.

Maybe all she needs to do is practise?

Every day, after school, Ella **practises** her ballet.

In her room, Ella bends her legs. Then she twirls—one twirl, two twirls, three twirls, just like Mrs Fry showed her.

Soon Ella is bending and twirling without falling over.

She shows her parents. One twirl, two twirls, three twirls! **Yay!**

Ella is ready for her next ballet class!

CHAPTER FIVE

'Hello, ballerinas,' Mrs Fry says. 'Please **welcome** our new ballet student.'

Next to Mrs Fry is . . . Alexander from school!

He walks over and stands next to Ella. Ella is so **happy** to see someone she knows!

'Hi, Alexander,' Ella says.

'Hi, Ella,' says Alexander. He wears one **spotty** sock and one **stripy** sock.

'I like your socks,' Ella says.

'I couldn't find the pairs,'
Alexander says.

'Did everybody practise?' Mrs Fry asks.

Ella nods. She bends her legs slowly. Then Ella begins to twirl. One twirl, two twirls . . . three twirls! Ella stays on her feet. She doesn't fall!

'Very good, Ella!' says Mrs Fry.

Everybody in the class **claps**. The other girls **smile** at Ella.

Ella is **proud**. She practised just like Nana Kate. And it worked!

'OK, class,' says Mrs Fry. 'It is time for some **free dancing**. I'll put on some music and you are allowed to dance in any way you like!'

The music fills the room. Ella and Alexander bust out their own dance moves!

Ella twirls and Alexander **spins** on his bottom.

'Nice twirls, Ella,' says a ballerina with curly hair.

After class, Ella runs over to Mum. 'I twirled without falling over!'

'I saw!' says Mum. 'Well done.'

Ella says **goodbye** to Alexander.

'See you next week, Ella,'
Alexander says.

Ella is so **excited**.
She can't wait
for her next
ballet class!

If you loved Meet ELLA, join her for more adventures!